CW00920719

The First Christmas
and Other Stories
From the New Testament

Look out for more life-affirming books
by Enid Blyton

Noah's Ark
and Other Stories from the Old Testament

The Land of Far Beyond

Enid Blyton®

The First Christmas
and Other Stories
From the
New Testament

Illustrated by Sam Loman

Hodder
Children's
Books

HODDER CHILDREN'S BOOKS

This collection copyright © Hodder and Stoughton Ltd, 2016
Illustrations by Sam Loman copyright © Hodder and Stoughton, 2016
Introduction © Pam Rhodes, 2016
Enid Blyton's signature is a Registered Trademark of
Hodder and Stoughton Ltd

These stories were first published by Macmillan Ltd in 1949,
as part of *The Enid Blyton Bible Stories* series, and reissued by
Grafton Books in 1986 as *Enid Blyton's Bible Stories*.

This edition published in 2016 by Hodder and Stoughton

The right of Enid Blyton to be identified as the Author of
the Work has been asserted by her in accordance with the
Copyright, Designs and Patents Act 1988

1 3 5 7 9 10 8 6 4 2

All rights reserved. Apart from any use permitted under UK copyright
law, this publication may only be reproduced, stored or transmitted,
in any form, or by any means with prior permission in writing from
the publishers or in the case of reprographic production in accordance
with the terms of licences issued by the Copyright Licensing Agency
and may not be otherwise circulated in any form of binding or cover
other than that in which it is published and without a similar
condition being imposed on the subsequent purchaser.

All characters and events in this publication, other than those clearly
in the public domain, are fictitious and any resemblance to real persons,
living or dead, is purely coincidental.

A Catalogue record for this book is available from the British Library.

ISBN 978 1 444 93281 2

Typeset in Caslon Twelve by AVon DataSet Ltd, Bidford-on-Avon, Warwickshire

Printed and bound in Great Britain by Clays Ltd, St Ives plc

MIX
Paper from
responsible sources
FSC
www.fsc.org
FSC® C104740

The paper and board used in this book are made from wood
from responsible sources

Hodder Children's Books
An imprint of Hachette Children's Group
Part of Hodder and Stoughton
Carmelite House, 50 Victoria Embankment,
London, EC4Y 0DZ

An Hachette UK Company
www.hachette.co.uk
www.hachettechildrens.co.uk

Contents

Introduction

I grew up on the stories of Enid Blyton. So did my children and grandchildren. In a prolific writing career that stretched from the nineteen twenties to the late sixties, Enid's tales of unforgettable characters in series like *The Famous Five*, *The Secret Seven*, *Malory Towers*, *Noddy* and *Brer Rabbit* have enchanted and entertained young readers around the world. She understood what children enjoy most in any story – excitement, intrigue, adventure, danger, and a satisfying explanation encapsulated in a great storyline that keeps them turning page after page.

So, when her mind was constantly brimming with her own fictional characters, what did Enid consider to be the most important story that children *needed* to hear? For her, that story should tell of 'the greatest figure the world has ever seen,' a man she described as 'a perfect hero, just, fearless and merciful.' That man is Jesus Christ, the Son of God, whose story is told in the Gospels of the New Testament, the second half of the Bible.

What worried Enid was the complexities of language and storylines in these ancient texts which are sometimes hard for adults, let alone children – so she set about rewriting some of the most important and memorable episodes from Christ's life with young readers in mind. She managed to keep the stories simple, reflecting the drama and beauty of the original text as closely as possible. In other hands, the end result might have been way above children's heads, but as the wonderful storyteller she was, these tales have the power to capture a child's imagination and interest from beginning to end.

In the Gospels, we hear Jesus explaining moral truths in parables, his own form of storytelling. In these, He teaches us to 'love one another', with helpful examples of goodness, kindness, unselfishness and justice. This book of Enid Blyton's retelling of Christ's own stories and the meaning of His time on earth, is full of love – Christ's love for us, our love for each other, and Enid's caring and timeless love for children everywhere.

Pam Rhodes

The First Christmas

Nearly two thousand years ago there lived in the town of Nazareth in Palestine a girl called Mary. One day an angel came to her with great news.

'Hail, Mary!' said the angel. 'I bring you great tidings. You will have a little baby boy, and you must call Him Jesus. He shall be great, and shall be called the Son of the Highest. He will be the Son of God, and of His kingdom there shall be no end.'

Now Mary was only a village girl, and she could hardly believe this news; but as she gazed up at the angel, she knew it was true. She was full of joy and wonder. She was to have a baby boy of her own, and He was to be the little Son of God.

Mary married a carpenter called Joseph, and

together they lived in a little house on the hillside. Her heart sang as she thought of the tiny baby who was to come to her that winter.

The summer went by, and it was autumn. Then the winter came – and with it arrived men who put up a big notice in the town. Mary went to read it.

It was a notice saying that everyone must go to their own home town and pay taxes. This meant that Mary and Joseph must leave Nazareth, and go to Bethlehem, for that was where their families had once lived.

'You shall ride on the donkey,' said Joseph. 'I will walk beside you. We shall be three or four days on the way, but the litte donkey will take you easily.'

So Mary and Joseph set off to go to Bethlehem. Mary rode on the little donkey, and Joseph walked beside her, leading it. Many other people were on the roads too, for everyone had to go to pay their taxes. Mary and Joseph travelled for some days, and one night Mary felt very tired.

'When shall we be there?' said Mary, 'I feel tired.

I want to lie down and rest.'

'There are the lights of Bethlehem,' said Joseph, pointing through the darkness to where some lights twinkled on a hilltop. 'We shall soon be there.'

'Shall we find room at Bethlehem?' said Mary. 'There are so many people going there.'

'We will go to an inn,' said Joseph. 'There you will find warmth and food, comfort and rest. We shall soon be there.'

When they climbed up the hill to the town of Bethlehem, Mary felt so tired that she longed to go to the inn at once.

'Here it is,' said Joseph, and he stopped the little donkey before a building that was well-lighted. Joseph called for the innkeeper, and a man came to the door, holding up a lantern so that he might see the travellers.

'Can you give us a room quickly?' said Joseph. 'My wife is very tired, and needs to rest at once.'

'My inn is full, and there is not a bed to be had in the whole town,' said the innkeeper. 'You will find nowhere to sleep. There is no room at the inn.'

'Can't you find us a resting place somewhere?' said Joseph, anxiously. 'My wife has come far and is so tired.'

The man swung his lantern up to look at Mary, who sat patiently on the donkey, waiting. He saw how tired she was, how white her face looked, and how patiently she sat there. He was filled with pity, and he wondered what he could do.

'I have a cave at the back of my inn, where my oxen sleep,' he said. 'Your wife could lie there. I will have it swept for you and new straw put down. But that is the best I can offer you.'

So Joseph said they would sleep in the cave that night, and he helped Mary off the donkey. She walked wearily round to the cave in the hillside, and saw the servant putting down piles of clean straw for her.

Mary lay down in the straw. Joseph looked after her tenderly. He brought her milk to drink, he made her a pillow of a rug, and he hung his cloak over the doorway so that the wind could be kept away.

Their little donkey was with them in the stable too. He ate his supper hungrily, looking round at Mary and Joseph as he munched. Mary smelt the nearby oxen, and felt the warmth their bodies made.

And that night Jesus was born to Mary, in the little stable at Bethlehem. Mary held Him closely in her arms, looking at Him with joy and love. The oxen looked round too, and the little donkey stared with large eyes. The doves watched and cooed softly. The little Son of God was there!

'Joseph, bring me the clothes I had with me,' said Mary. 'I thought perhaps the baby would be born whilst we travelled and I brought His swaddling clothes with me.'

In those far-off days the first clothes a baby wore were called his swaddling clothes. He was wrapped round and round in a long piece of linen cloth. Mary took the linen from Joseph, and wrapped the baby in His swaddling clothes. Then she wondered where to put Him, for she wanted to sleep.

'He cannot lie on this straw,' said Mary, anxiously.

'Oh, Joseph, we have no cradle for our little baby.'

'See,' said Joseph, 'there is a manger here full of soft hay. It will be a cradle for Him.'

Joseph put the tiny child into the manger, laying Him down carefully in the soft hay. How small He was! How downy His hair was, and how tiny His fingers were with their pink nails!

Then Mary, tired out, fell asleep on the straw, whilst Joseph kept watch beside her, and the baby slept peacefully in the manger nearby. The lantern light flickered when the wind stole in, and sometimes the oxen stamped on the floor.

That was the first Christmas, the birthday of the little Christ Child. The little Son of God was born, the great teacher of the world – but only Joseph and Mary knew that at last He had come.

No bells rang out at His birth. The people in the inn slept soundly, not guessing that the Son of God was in a nearby stable.

But the angels in heaven knew the great happening. They must spread the news. They must come to our world and tell someone. They had kept watch over the city of Bethlehem that night, and they were filled with joy to know that the little Son of God was born.

The Shepherds in the Night

Who was awake to hear the angels' news? There was no one in the town awake that night, but on the hillside outside Bethlehem there were some shepherds, watching their sheep.

They talked quietly together. They had much to talk about that night, for they had watched hundreds of people walking and riding by their quiet fields, on the way to pay their taxes at Bethlehem. It was seldom that the shepherds saw so many people.

As the shepherds talked, looking round at their quiet sheep, a very strange thing happened. The sky became bright, and a great light appeared in it, and shone all round them. The shepherds were surprised and frightened. What was this brilliant light that shone in the darkness of the night?

They looked up fearfully. Then in the middle of the dazzling light they saw a beautiful angel. He shone too, and he spoke to them in a voice that sounded like mighty music.

'See,' said one shepherd to another in wonder. 'An angel.'

They all fell upon their knees, and some covered their faces with their cloaks, afraid of the dazzling light. They were trembling.

Then the voice of the angel came upon the hillside, full of joy and happiness.

'Fear not; for behold I bring you good tidings of great joy, which shall be to all people. For unto you is born this day in the city of David a Saviour, which is Christ the Lord. And this shall be a sign unto you – you shall find the babe wrapped in swaddling clothes and lying in a manger.'

The shepherds listened in the greatest wonder. They gazed at the angel in awe, and listened to this wonderful being with his great overshadowing wings.

As they looked, another strange thing happened, which made the shepherds tremble even more.

The dark sky disappeared, and in its place came a crowd of shining beings, bright as the sun, filling the whole sky. Everywhere the shepherds looked there were angels, singing joyfully.

'Glory to God in the highest,' sang the host of angels, 'and on Earth peace, goodwill towards men.'

Over and over again the angels sang these words, and the shepherds, amazed, afraid and wondering, listened and marvelled. Surely all the angels in heaven were over Bethlehem that night.

Then, as the shepherds watched, the dazzling light slowly faded away, and the darkness of the night came back. The angels vanished with the light, and then the sky was quite dark again, set with twinkling stars that had been outshone by the glory of the angels. A sheep bleated and a dog barked. There was nothing to show that heaven had opened to the shepherds that night.

The frightened men were silent for a time, and

then they began to talk in low voices that gradually became louder.

'They were angels. How dazzling they were! We saw angels. They came to us, the shepherds on the hillside.'

'It couldn't have been a dream. Nobody could dream like that.'

'I was frightened. I hardly dared to look at the angels at first.'

'Why did they come to us? Why should they choose men like us to sing to?'

'You heard what the first angel said – he said a Saviour had been born to us, Christ the Lord. He said that He was born in the City of David tonight – that means in Bethlehem, for Bethlehem is the City of David!'

'Can it be true?'

'We will go and find the little King. I want to see Him.'

'We cannot go at midnight. And how do we know where He is?'

'Why should the Holy Child be put in a manger? Surely He should have a cradle!'

'He must have been born to one of the late travellers, who could find no room at the inn. They must have had to put Him in a manger. I am going to see.'

The shepherds, excited and full of great wonder, went up the hillside to Bethlehem. They left their dogs to guard the sheep, all but one who went with them.

Soon they came to the inn, and, at the back, where the stable was built into the hillside cave, they saw a light. 'Let us go to the stable and see if the Son of God is there,' whispered one shepherd. So, treading softly, they went round to the back of the inn, and came to the entrance of the stable. Across it was stretched Joseph's rough cloak to keep out the wind. The shepherds peered over it into the stable.

They saw what the angel had told them – a babe wrapped in swaddling clothes, lying in a manger!

On the straw, asleep, was Mary. Nearby was

Joseph, keeping watch over her and the child.

'There's the baby,' whispered the shepherds, in excitement. 'In the manger, wrapped in swaddling clothes. There is the Saviour, the little Son of God.'

Mary heard what they said. She lifted the child from the manger and took Him on her knee. The shepherds knelt down before Him and worshipped Him. Again and again they told the wondering Mary all that had happened.

The oxen stared, and the dog pressed close to his master, wondering at the strange happenings of the night. Then, seeing that Mary was looking tired, the shepherds went at last, walking softly in the night.

'We will tell everyone the news tomorrow!' said the shepherds. 'Everyone. What will they say when they know that whilst they slept we have seen angels?'

Down the hill they went, back to their sheep, sometimes looking up into the sky to see if an angel might once again appear. All through that night they talked eagerly of the angels, the Holy Child in the stable, and of Mary, His gentle mother.

The next day they told everyone of what had happened to them in the night, and many people went to peep in at the stable, to see the little child.

Mary held Him close to her, and thought often of the angel she herself had seen nine months before. She thought of the excited shepherds, and the host of shining angels they too had seen and heard. Her baby was the little Son of God. Mary could hardly believe such a thing was true.

The Three Wise Men

Far far away from Bethlehem in a land that lay to the east, there lived some wise and learned men. At night these men studied the stars in the heavens. They said that the stars showed them the great thoughts of God. They said that when a new star appeared, it was God's way of telling men that some great thing was happening in the world.

Then, one night, a new star appeared in the sky, when the wise men were watching. The second night the star was brighter still. The third night it was so dazzling that its light seemed to put out the twinkling of the other stars.

'God has sent this star to say that something wonderful is happening,' said the wise men. 'We will look in our old, old book, where wisdom is kept, and we will find out what this star means.'

So they studied their old wise books, and they found in them a tale of a great King who was to be born into the world to rule over it. He was to be King of the Jews, and ruler of the world.

'The star seems to stand over Israel, the kingdom of the Jews,' said one wise man. 'This star must mean that the great King is born at last. We will go to worship Him, for our books say He will be the greatest King in the world.'

'We will take Him presents of gold and frankincense and myrrh,' said another. 'We will tell our servants to make ready to go with us.'

So, a little while later, when the star was still brilliant every night in the sky, the three wise men set off on their camels. They were like kings in their own country, and a long train of servants followed behind on swift-footed camels.

They travelled for many days and nights, and always at night the great star shone before them to guide them on their way.

They came at last to the land of Israel, where the little Jesus had been born. They went, of course, to the city where the Jewish King lived, thinking that surely the new little King would be there, in the palace of Jerusalem.

Herod was the King there, and he was a wicked man. When his servants came running to tell him that three rich men, seated on magnificent camels, with a train of servants behind them, were at the gates of the palace, Herod bade his servants bring them before him.

The wise men went to see Herod. They looked strange and most kingly in their turbans and flowing robes. They asked Herod a question that amazed and angered him.

'Where is the child who is born King of the Jews?' they asked. 'His star has gone before us in the east, and we wish to worship Him. Where is He?'

'I am the King,' said Herod, full of anger. 'What is this child you talk of? And what is this star?'

The wise men told him all they knew. 'We are

certain that a great King has been born,' they said, 'and we must find Him. Can you not tell us where He is?'

Herod sat silent for a moment. Who was this newborn King these rich strangers spoke of? Herod was quite certain they were speaking the truth. He could see that these men were learned, and knew far more than he did.

'I will find out where this newborn King is, and kill him,' thought Herod to himself. 'But this I will not tell these men. They shall go to find the child for me, and tell me where he is – then I will send my soldiers to kill him.'

So Herod spoke craftily to the wise men. 'I will find out what you want to know. I have wise men in my court who know the sayings of long ago Jews, who said that in due time a great King would be born. Perhaps this is the child you mean.'

Then Herod sent for his own wise men and bade them look in the books they had to see what was said of a great King to be born to the Jews. The learned men looked and they found what they wanted to know.

'The King will be born in the city of Bethlehem,' they said.

'Where is that?' asked the wise men.

'Not far away,' said Herod. 'It will not take you long to get there.'

'We will go now,' said the three wise men, and they turned to go. But Herod stopped them.

'Wait,' he said, 'when you find this newborn King, come back here to tell me where he is, for I too would worship Him.'

The wise men did not know that Herod meant to kill the little King, and not to worship Him. 'You shall be told where He is,' they said. 'We will return here and tell you.'

Then they mounted their camels and went to find the city of Bethlehem, which, as Herod had said, was not far away.

The sun set, and once again the brilliant star flashed into the sky. It seemed to stand exactly over the town of Bethlehem. The strangers, with their train of servants, went up the hill to Bethlehem, their

harness jingling and their jewelled turbans and cloaks flashing in the brilliant light of the great star.

They passed the wondering shepherds, and went into the little city. They stopped to ask a woman to guide them.

'Can you tell us where to find a newborn child?' they asked.

The woman stared at these rich strangers in surprise. She felt sure they must want to know where Jesus was, for everyone knew how angels had come to proclaim His birth.

'Yes,' she said, 'you will find the baby in the house yonder. He was born in the stable of the inn, because there was no room for Him – but now that the travellers have left the city, room was found for His parents at that house. You will find Him there with His mother.'

The star seemed to stand right over the house to which the woman pointed. The wise men felt sure it was the right one. They made their way to it, riding on their magnificent camels.

The Angel's Warning

When Mary saw these three grandly dressed men kneeling before her tiny baby, she was amazed. Angels had come to proclaim His birth, shepherds had worshipped Him – and now here were three great men kneeling before Him.

'We have found the little King,' said one wise man. 'We have brought Him kingly presents. Here is gold for Him, a gift for a King.'

'And here is sweet-smelling frankincense,' said another.

'And I bring Him myrrh, rare and precious,' said the third.

These were indeed kingly gifts, and Mary looked at them in wonder, holding the baby closely against her. He was her own child, but He seemed to belong to many others too – to the angels in heaven, to the simple shepherds in the fields, to wise and rich men of far countries. He had been born for the whole world, not only for her.

The wise men left and went to stay for the night at the inn. There was room for them, because the many travellers who had come to the little city had left some time before.

'Tomorrow we will go back to Herod and tell him where the newborn King is, so that he may come and worship Him,' said the wise men.

But in the night God sent dreams to them, to warn them not to return to Herod, but to go back to their country another way.

So they mounted their camels, and returned to their country without going near Jerusalem, where Herod lived.

In vain Herod waited for the three wise men to return. His servants soon found out that they had been to Bethlehem but had returned home another way. This made Herod so angry that he hardly knew what he was doing.

First he sent his soldiers after the wise men to stop them, but they were too far away. Then he made up his mind to find the newborn baby and kill Him.

But no one knew where the child was, nor did anyone even know how old He might be. The wise men themselves had not known how old the baby was. Herod sat on his throne, his heart black and angry.

'Call my soldiers to me,' he said at last.

They came before him, and Herod gave them a cruel and terrible command.

'Go to the town of Bethlehem and kill every boy child there who is under two years old,' he said. 'Go to the villages round about and kill the young baby boys there too. Let no one escape.'

The soldiers rode off, their harnesses jingling loudly. They rode up the hill to Bethlehem, and once again the quiet shepherds stared in wonder at strange visitors. But soon, alas, they heard the screams and cries of the mothers whose little sons had been killed, and they knew that something dreadful was happening.

Every boy child was killed by the cruel soldiers, and when their terrible work was done, they rode down the hills again, past the watching shepherds, to tell Herod that his commands had been obeyed.

'There is no boy child under two years old left in Bethlehem or the villages nearby,' said the captain of the soldiers, and Herod was well pleased.

'The newborn King is dead,' he thought. 'I have been clever, I have killed the baby who might one day have been greater than I am.'

But Jesus was not killed. He was safe. On the night that the wise men had left Mary, the little family had gone to bed, and were asleep. But, as Joseph slept, an angel came to him in his dreams, and spoke to him.

'Arise,' said the shining angel. 'Take the young Child and His mother, and flee into Egypt, and stay there until I tell you to return; for Herod will seek the young Child to destroy Him.'

Joseph awoke at once. He sat up. The angel was gone, but the words he had said still sounded in Joseph's ears. Joseph knew that there was danger near, and he awoke Mary at once.

'We must make ready and go,' he said, and he told her what the angel had said. Then Mary knew they must go, and she went to put her few things into a bundle, and to lift up the baby Jesus. Joseph went to get the little donkey, and soon, in the silence of the night, the four of them fled away secretly.

They went as quickly as they could, longing to pass over into the land of Egypt, which did not belong to Herod. He would have no power over them there.

So, when Herod's soldiers came a little later to the city of Bethlehem, Jesus was not there. He was safe in Egypt, where Herod could not reach Him.

And there, until it was safe for Him to return to His own country, the little newborn King lived and grew strong and kind and loving. No one knew He was a King. His father was a carpenter, and His friends were the boys of the villages around.

But His mother knew. Often she remembered the tale of the shepherds who had seen the angels in the sky, and she remembered too the three wise men who had come to kneel before her baby. She still had the wonderful presents they had given to her for Him. He would one day be the greatest King in the world.

But it was not by power or riches or might that the baby in the stable grew to be the greatest man the world has ever seen. It was by something greater than all these – by LOVE alone.

That is the story of the first Christmas, which we remember to this day, and which we keep with joy and delight.

The Little Boy Jesus

When Jesus was a baby, His mother and father had to take Him away from Bethlehem, because King Herod had told his soldiers to kill all the boy babies there.

'We will go to the town of Nazareth,' said Joseph. 'Our friends are there. We shall be happy in our own land.'

And so one day the little company arrived at Nazareth, set high up on the green hillside.

'Now we are home again,' said Mary, gladly. 'See how the little white houses shine in the sun. We will have one of those to live in, Joseph, and our little Jesus shall grow up here in the sunshine, and learn to help you in your shop.'

So Jesus was brought up in one of the little white houses on the hillside. It was made of sun-dried bricks, and He helped Joseph to whitewash it each year, so that it shone clean and white.

In this little house Joseph set up his carpenter's shop. Mary and Jesus liked to hear all the hammering and sawing that went on. Jesus often went into the shop and watched his father. He sometimes lifted a heavy hammer, and played with the big and little nails.

'One day I will help you,' He told Joseph. 'I shall be a carpenter too.'

Jesus did all the things that the other children of Nazareth did. He went to fetch water from the well for His mother in the old stone pitcher. Even today the people of Nazareth see the same old well, where once, years ago, a bright-eyed boy called Jesus came to fetch water and to talk to the other children there.

Jesus wandered over the hillside too, and picked flowers for his mother. The hillside was covered with them in spring and summer. Jesus talked with the shepherds too, and heard their tales. He played with the lambs, listened to the birds singing, and watched the sower sowing his seed in the fields.

His mother told him many stories. You know them too. She told Him how God made the world. He heard about the Garden of Eden and how Adam and Eve were sent away from it. He liked hearing about Noah and his ark, and He loved the rainbow when He saw it in the sky, and remembered how God had set it there as a promise never to flood the world again.

He knew the stories of the giant Samson, of David and Goliath, and Daniel in the lions' den. Mary taught him to obey God's commands, and to pray to Him each day. Jesus listened eagerly, and learnt everything His mother could tell Him.

When He was old enough He, like you, went to school. He had to learn His lessons – and He had to learn something else too. He had to learn the law of God, and this was very difficult.

The law of God had been written down by Jewish teachers, and they had filled books full of tiny laws as well as big ones. The tiny laws told people exactly how they should wash a plate, and arrange their clothes, and things like that. When Jesus saw that the people sometimes thought more of doing these small things correctly than they did of such big things as being kind and generous to one another, He was puzzled.

'Surely it is better to be like old Sarah, who lives down the hill and is always kind to everyone in trouble – though she forgets the little commands – than it is to be like James, who never forgets the little things, but is unjust and unkind all the time,' thought Jesus.

He was only a boy then, but He thought things out for Himself. He prayed to God to show Him what was really right and good.

'One day I shall know these things,' He said to Himself. 'I shall know enough to tell others what I think. I shall be able to teach them and help them. That is the thing I want to do most of all.'

Twelve Years Old

Once each year the Jewish people kept a great feast or holiday. They liked to go to Jerusalem, where their beautiful Temple was built. Joseph and Mary loved to go too.

'What do you do there when you go?' asked Jesus.

'There are meetings and services,' said Mary. 'And we meet many people there, and see old friends. It is an exciting and happy time. When you are twelve we will take you with us, Jesus.'

So, when He was twelve years old, His mother kept her promise. 'You can come with us,' she said. 'You are a big boy now – and it is time that you went to the Temple with us and became one of the members of the church. You must promise to keep the law, you know.'

It was very exciting to think of such a long journey. Jesus had heard so much of Jerusalem and the Temple. Now He was really going to see it.

'I shall walk down strange roads, I shall see hundreds of people. At night we shall camp out by the wayside, and see the stars shining above us,' He thought. 'And perhaps I shall be able to talk to learned and wise men in the Temple and ask them some of the things I want so much to know.'

The great day came. Joseph and Mary were ready to go. Joseph had finished all the work he had to do and Mary had tidied up the house. Everything was ready. Joseph shut the door of the little house, and smiled to see Jesus's excited face.

Other children were going too. They ran to join Jesus. They all liked this wise, kindly boy and the things He said and did.

'Walk with us!' they cried. 'We're going down the hill and across the plain – and then we cross the river Jordan. Come along!'

It was a lovely journey over the hills and plains to Jerusalem. Jesus felt the spring sun warm on His shoulders, He heard the birds singing, and saw the thousands of flowers under His feet.

There was plenty to see on the way. Each day was exciting – and the nights were even more exciting. For them camp fires were made, meals were cooked, and old songs and hymns were sung by the hundreds of people in the little camps.

Jesus liked to watch all the lights from the camp fires. He liked to lie on His back and look up at the brilliant stars. He liked to hear the singing.

Then at last they came to Jerusalem, and went to the Holy Temple. Jesus stood and looked at the beautiful building.

'That is the house of God, my Heavenly Father,' He thought. 'He dwells there. I am going to His house.'

Jesus was taken into the Temple. God felt very near to Him there. He was taken before the wise men of the Temple, and they made Him a member of the church.

'Now you must count yourself grown-up,' said the wise men. 'You must keep all the laws of the church.'

And then the great Feast was over. The holiday was ended. It was time to go home.

'Here are our things for you to carry, Joseph,' said Mary. 'How lovely it has been to meet all our old friends again! How good to know that Jesus belongs to our church! And how nice it will be to be back home again in our own little house!'

Mary did not see Jesus all that day. She wondered where He was. Perhaps He was with the other boys. She must count Him as grown-up now, and let Him go away on His own. But where could He be?

'He is sure to come and look for us when we camp tonight,' she thought. But the night came, and there was no Jesus.

'We must look for Him, Joseph,' said Mary, anxiously. 'Go and ask the other boys if they know where He is.'

'No,' said the boys. 'We haven't seen Him at all.

He didn't walk with us.'

Nobody knew where Jesus was. Not one person had seen Him since they had left Jerusalem. Mary and Joseph were very worried.

'We will go back to Jerusalem,' said Joseph.

So back they went. But still they could not find Jesus. He was not at the house where they had stayed. Nobody could tell them anything about Him.

Jerusalem was a big city. Mary and Joseph hardly knew where to look. For three days they went up and down the streets, asking everyone they met the same question. 'Have you seen our boy Jesus?'

'There is only one place left to look,' said Mary, at last. 'And that is the Temple itself. He loved the Temple, Joseph. He wanted to ask the wise men so many questions, and there was no time. Perhaps He has gone back to the Temple.'

They went to see – and there they found Jesus. He had not been wandering about the great city, playing, or looking at the strange sights. He had been in the temple all the time, an earnest, urgent little boy, anxious to find out all He could about God and His commands.

He had found the wise men, the ones who knew more about the Jewish law than anyone in the land. He had asked them questions – questions they did not know how to answer! They were amazed at this young boy who knew so much about the law of God – why, He knew more than they did!

They kept Him there hour after hour, asking Him questions too. Jesus forgot everything except that now at last He was finding out things He needed to know. He felt close to God in the Temple, He felt that His Heavenly Father had welcomed him, that He was really and truly His son.

Perhaps in those three strange days, when He was talking so earnestly with the wise and learned men, Jesus felt for the first time His great power for doing good. He listened to all the wise men said, turning their long words into simple ones in His mind, seeing how easy it would be to tell the common people these things in simple language and stories.

Here, in the Temple, He belonged to God, more than He belonged to Joseph and Mary. He stood there in the midst of all the wise men, and they marvelled at His knowledge and wisdom.

And then He suddenly saw His parents nearby, looking at Him with anxious, troubled eyes! Mary went to Him, weeping with joy.

'Son!' she said. 'Why have you behaved like this? Your father and I have been looking for you everywhere. We have been so worried.'

Jesus was surprised. 'But did you not guess where I would be?' He said. 'I had to come to my Father's house, and learn the things I should know.'

He went home with Mary and Joseph. He became their young boy again, and obeyed them in all things. He was wise and He was wonderful, but the time had not yet come when He could do exactly as He wanted to.

So He settled down again in Nazareth, and pondered over all the things He had learnt in the Temple. He knew that wisdom and understanding could only grow slowly, and He was content to live with His family, helping His father and mother, until the right time came.

The Twelve Disciples

At last the time came when Jesus knew He must start preaching to His people, and helping them in all the many ways He could.

But it would be difficult for one man alone to do this. 'I must have friends who will help me,' thought Jesus. 'I must have disciples – men I can teach so that they may themselves go out and teach others. But they must be good men, men I can love and trust.'

He went to walk beside the lovely lake of Galilee. Fishermen were at work there, some fishing, some mending nets, and some mending their boats. Jesus watched them, looking closely at each man's face as He passed by.

He saw a boat in which were two brothers, Simon

and Andrew. They were good men and good fishermen. Their faces were open and honest. Jesus felt He could trust men like these.

He called to them across the shimmering blue water. 'Come with me!' He said. 'I will make you fishers of men!'

This was a strange thing to say, and Simon and Andrew did not understand the words at all. Not for some time did they know that Jesus meant them to go out with Him and catch men to bring them into His kingdom of love. Now they stood up in their boat and looked at the man who called to them.

There was something in His face that made them go to Him. Such goodness shone out of it that they felt they must do what this man said. They rowed to the shore at once and joined Jesus.

There were two other brothers in another boat, mending their nets. Jesus called to them as well. 'Come with me!'

The two brothers came eagerly to this man with

the beautiful face. Now Jesus had four friends to help Him, four good men to do as He said, and to love Him and trust Him.

He needed twelve, so He chose eight more. But the four He had chosen first were the closest of all to Him.

One of them was an eager, lovable man, a man who could be kind and brave and loving – but he could be untrustworthy too, and do things he was ashamed of afterwards. That was Simon – and Jesus knew both the good and the bad in Simon, but He loved him and knew that the good would be more powerful than the bad.

Jesus looked at Simon. 'Your name is Simon,' He said, 'But I shall call you Peter.'

'Why is that?' asked Peter, surprised.

'Because the name Peter means a rock,' said Jesus. 'I have a great kingdom to build, Peter, and it must be built on rock, not sand. You shall be Peter, a rock, and my Kingdom will depend a great deal on you.'

The twelve disciples followed Jesus everywhere, loving Him and worshipping Him, a very happy company of men.

Jesus began His great and wonderful work. Soon His name was on everyone's lips.

'Have you heard what that man Jesus says? You should go to hear Him preach!'

'You can understand every single word He says! He speaks so simply. He tells us that God is our Heavenly Father who loves us and cares for us. He says we are to trust Him and fear nothing.'

'We must turn from evil and do good. We must pray and be kind and loving. I have never heard such preaching before.'

'The children love Him! They follow Him everywhere. He tells such wonderful stories, you see, that even the little ones can understand. My little boy is always going to hear Him.'

'Don't you think His face is goodness itself? Goodness should only be preached by a man like that! The other preachers I have heard never make me

want to be good as this man does. It's because He's so good Himself.'

'Do you know who He is? He's only Jesus, the son of the carpenter at Nazareth! And yet He is greater and better than anyone I have ever known!'

So the people talked of Him, loving Him, crowding to hear Him in the churches when He preached, gathering round Him on the hills when He talked to them, bringing their children to Him because He loved them and understood them.

And then other things began to be said.

'Listen! Have you heard what Jesus did to old Anna? You know she was so ill? Well, He touched her and made her better! She is walking about again!'

'Have you heard about little John? His foot was always bad, and he couldn't walk on it. His mother took him to Jesus, and He took the boy into his arms and stroked the bad foot gently – and now the child can walk!'

'He does miracles! He is so good that He can do wonders. He is truly the Son of God.'

'Wherever He goes He comforts and heals and brings happiness. His eyes shine with goodness. His hands are full of healing power. Twice have I seen Him, and I have said I will never do a wrong thing again. I felt that I *must* be good when I heard Him preaching.'

'It is both soul and body He heals and makes well. Let us go and hear Him today. We will take the children too, because He loves them so.'

The disciples went about with Jesus, marvelling at His great gifts of healing, listening to His wonderful stories, told in such simple words, helping Him, and caring for Him when He was tired.

And everywhere He went the people flocked round Him, anxious even to touch just the hem of His robe.

'Goodness flows out of Him!' they said. 'Truly He is the Son of God!'

The Nobleman's Son

Now, in the town of Capernaum there lived a nobleman, who had a little son.

The father loved his little boy with all his heart, and petted him and gave him servants to wait on him. But one day the boy fell ill.

'Get the doctor,' said the nobleman, anxiously. 'The child is hot – he will not play or eat. He is ill!'

The doctor came. 'Send him to bed,' he said. 'He will soon be better.'

But the child didn't get better, but much worse. The father sent for more and more doctors, but the little boy steadily grew worse. The nobleman spoke anxiously to the doctors round the bed.

'What can we do? See, he will die if we do not do

something quickly.'

The doctors looked sadly at the nobleman. His son was dying already, and there was nothing they could do. The father rose up in sorrow, for he saw what they did not dare to say. He went into his own room, full of grief and sadness.

His servants came to him.

'Sir,' said one, timidly, 'we love your son, so we have come to tell you of a new and wonderful doctor. He is a preacher and a healer. We have heard marvellous tales of His doings. Could you not ask Him to see your son?'

'Where is this man?' said the nobleman.

'At Cana in Galilee,' answered the servant. 'Shall I fetch Him for you?'

'No, I will go myself,' said the nobleman. He went quickly to say goodbye to the small, restless boy, and then he set out for Cana.

He met people who told him where to find Jesus. 'He is there in that house,' said a woman, pointing. 'He is not only a healer. He is the Son of God, and

He is the most wonderful preacher we ever heard.'

The nobleman did not care about that – all he wanted was a doctor who could make his precious son better. He went into the house and asked for Jesus.

Jesus came into the room where he waited, and looked at the anxious man. The nobleman trusted Him at once, because of the goodness that shone from His face. He felt His power, and was quite sure that this man could cure his son.

'Sir, my little boy lies ill at Capernaum,' he said. 'The doctors fear that he is dying. You can make him better again. Will you come back with me?'

Jesus listened, and wondered if this man, like many others, had come just to see Him do a miracle. A great many people followed Him simply to watch Him doing wonders – and then they said that truly He was the Son of God! But Jesus did not want them to watch for miracles and believe in Him because of those – He wanted them to believe the things He told them, and to make their hearts clean and be good.

He spoke sadly to the nobleman. 'You and the others only want to see me doing wonderful things. You will not believe the things I say unless I do a miracle.'

'Oh, sir, I want neither signs nor wonders,' said the nobleman, in despair. 'All I want is for you to come back with me now and see if you can make my child better. He will surely die – and I love him so!'

Jesus looked at the anxious father. He was sorry for him, and pitied him in his great grief.

He spoke to him gently. 'Do not be afraid,' He said. 'Your son lives. Go home again, and you will see that my words are true.'

The nobleman believed Jesus at once. He felt a great joy filling his heart. His child was better! He wasn't going to die! This man had said so, and a man with a face of such goodness could speak only the truth.

It didn't matter at all that Jesus was not going back with him, was not even going to see his child.

It didn't matter that He had only spoken a few words, and had not put His hands on the little boy to heal him. The father was sure that his son was better.

'This man has such a power for good that somehow He can reach out and heal my child even though he is far away!' thought the man.

He left the house at once and was soon on his way back home.

He came near his house, and saw his servants watching for him. Their faces were full of joy, and they waved to him as he came near. They ran to meet him, shouting loudly.

'Your son is well! He comes to welcome you!'

A servant came out of the house with the little boy. 'I'm better, my father,' said the child. 'I will play a game with you. I am quite better.'

The nobleman took his son into his arms, so full of thankfulness that at first he could hardly speak. He held his child tightly, feeling that he could never let him go.

He looked up at his smiling servants at last.

'Tell me,' he said, 'what time did the child begin to feel better?'

'Sir, he was about to die,' said a servant. 'He lay on his bed at the point of death – and then, at seven, the fever left him, and he was better.'

'At seven!' said the nobleman, amazed and glad. 'That was the moment when Jesus said to me, 'Your son lives!' It was the exact moment, I knew that His power would heal him. Oh, my son, you are well again!'

'Did you see the wonderful doctor then?' asked the servants, pressing around. 'What did He do? What did He say?'

'You should all go to hear Him preach,' said the nobleman. 'And each one of us must do what He says. We will believe in Him, and obey all His commands, however difficult they may be.'

'I shall go to Him too,' said the little boy. 'I want to see Him. I want to hear His stories.'

And so, in yet another household there were many who loved Jesus, and believed all he said. The little boy loved Him most of all, and tried to get as near Jesus as he could whenever he told one of His stories.

'Jesus healed me,' he told everyone proudly. 'He made me well again.'

The Loaves and the Fishes

There was once a small boy who lived up in the hills that rose above the Lake of Galilee. He lived in a little white house with his mother and father and little sister. He was quite an ordinary little boy, who didn't dream that one day something wonderful was going to happen to him.

He helped his father on the hills, and he fetched water for his mother and sometimes looked after his little sister. Often he went fishing by himself, catching the fish in his hands, for he had no net.

One day he caught two little fish, and he was very proud of himself. He took them to his mother.

'Will you pickle these for me?' he asked her. She smiled at him.

'Yes, I will pickle them for you,' she said. 'And you shall eat them tomorrow. There will only be enough for you because they are so small.'

So she pickled the two little fish and put them aside for the boy.

Now the next day the little boy was out on the hills with his little sister when he suddenly saw a great many people. They were streaming along the roads that led to the country round about the village of Bethsaida. The little boy had never seen so many people in the hills before.

He was astonished. Where had they all come from? And why were they there? Had something happened?

'I'm going to ask what's happened,' the boy told his sister. 'Stay here till I come back. What hundreds of people there are!'

He ran off to the crowds. 'What's happened?' he asked. 'Why have you all come here? There is nobody about here usually, except the villagers.'

'We're looking for Jesus,' said a woman. 'He set

off in His boat across the lake with His disciples. So we've walked round the lake to find Him. He must be somewhere here. Have you seen Him?'

'Who is Jesus?' asked the little boy.

'Oh, haven't you heard of Him?' said another boy. 'He's a wonderful man. He can do miracles and wonders! He can, really! He makes sick people well again and He can even make dead people alive. And there's another thing – He can tell the most marvellous stories. That's why *I've* come today. I love stories.'

'So do I,' said the boy from the hills. 'I wish I could see this wonderful man and hear His stories. I think I'll go and ask my mother if I may.'

He ran off home, and rushed into the house so fast that his mother looked up in surprise.

'Mother! Have you heard of a man called Jesus?' panted the boy. 'He's somewhere in the hills nearby today. You should see the crowds that have come to hear Him! Mother, may I go and hear Him too? He tells stories and does miracles. I do so want to see Him.'

'Very well,' said his mother, smiling at the excited little boy. 'Just wait a minute, though, and let me pack you up some food to take with you. Look, here are five little loaves you can have – and wouldn't you like to take the two little fish you caught yesterday, that I have pickled for you?'

The boy could hardly wait for his mother to put his food into a small basket. He took it from her, said goodbye and ran off quickly.

The crowds were even bigger when he got up to them. 'Is Jesus here?' he asked, anxiously. 'I haven't missed Him, have I?'

'He's over on that grassy hillside,' said a man. 'His disciples are with Him.'

Yes, Jesus was there. He had really come to these hills for a rest, because He was tired. But when He saw the crowds streaming along, He was sorry for them.

'They are like sheep without a shepherd,' He said to His disciples, and He went to meet the people.

The little boy suddenly saw Him. He knew

without a doubt that it was Jesus. He had never seen such clear, steady eyes before, such a wonderful face, or heard such a voice. So that was Jesus, the man of wonders and miracles! The little boy took a deep breath, and gazed at Him in awe and wonder.

If only he could do something for this man! He was a hero to the little boy. If only Jesus would look at him and smile at him! But Jesus had so many people to see to, so much to do, that He didn't even look in the small boy's direction.

The disciples went here and there among the crowds, looking for sick, lame or blind people to bring to Jesus. The little boy saw them taken to Him, saw Him put His hands on them, and talk to them.

And behold they were well again, they could see, they could walk and run! They broke into shouts and songs of joy, and went down the hill, praising God and telling everyone what had happened to them.

Then Jesus sat down and began to preach. The little boy listened. Jesus told some of His stories, and the lad strained his ears so that he should not miss a word.

'What wonderful stories!' he thought. 'I can understand them all! I shall remember each one, and tell them to my mother and my little sister. They will love them.'

Jesus left His seat on the grassy hillside and went among the crowd, talking and healing once more. The boy followed Him at a distance, never losing sight of Him. What a wonderful day this was – so many people, so much to see – and this marvellous man in the middle of it all!

The boy had forgotten all about the food in the little basket his mother had given him. Usually he was very hungry and ate everything far too soon when he came out for the day. But today he had forgotten even to eat.

The day went by and the sun began to sink. Hundreds of people were still there in the hills, excited and happy. But they were beginning to get tired now, and most of them were very hungry, for they had not brought any food with them. They had walked a very long way, and now that they were hungry they wondered if there was anywhere to buy food. But there were no shops in the hills.

The disciples went to Jesus. 'Master,' they said, 'shall we send these people away and tell them to go into the villages and buy bread?'

'We must feed them,' said Jesus.

'But Master – it would cost more than two hundred shillings to buy food for so many,' said Philip, who was in charge of the money that the disciples had. 'Do you wish us to go and buy food for the crowds?'

'Has no one here any food?' said Jesus. 'Go and see.' So the disciples went round the hillside, asking the same question over and over again.

'Has anyone food here? Who has brought food? Has anyone food here?'

But the people shook their heads. Either they had eaten what little they had brought, or they had forgotten to bring any in their excitement.

'Has anyone food here?' came the voices of the disciples, and the little boy heard the question too. He suddenly remembered the basket of food he had brought – the five little loaves and the two small fishes. He unwrapped them from the cloth in the basket and looked at them.

'I would so much like to give them to Jesus,' thought the small boy. 'I do so want to do something for Him, even if it's only a small thing. But would I dare to give these loaves and fishes to the disciples?'

He suddenly made up his mind. Yes, he would at least offer his food. So he pushed his way through the crowd and went up to one of the disciples.

'I have a little bread,' he said. 'And look, there are two small fishes as well. You can have them.'

The disciple took the basket, and led the boy up to Jesus.

'Master,' he said, 'there is a lad here with five loaves and two fishes.'

The boy was delighted to be so near the wonderful man he had been watching all the day. He looked up at Him shyly, his eyes wide with pleasure. Jesus smiled at him and took the basket from the disciple.

'Tell the people to sit down in companies of fifty so that we may feed them easily,' He said to His disciples. The people obeyed, sitting down in big groups. The little boy watched in wonder. What was Jesus going to do?

Jesus took the five loaves from the basket and broke them. He looked up to heaven and blessed the bread He had broken. He gave it to His disciples. Then He divided the little fish and gave those to them as well.

The disciples came up one by one to get the food, and to the little boy's wonder and amazement, Jesus always had plenty for them.

He went on breaking up the bread and the fishes, giving out more and more, and the disciples came up time and again for another share to give to the hungry people.

'There is no end to my bread and fishes!' thought the little boy. 'How can so little become so much?

This is a miracle I am watching. Jesus is doing a miracle with my five little loaves and two little fishes!'

There were five thousand people sitting on the hills and they were all fed. The disciples sat down to eat at last, and Jesus sat too, with the small boy beside Him eating his own share, marvelling at every mouthful he took.

'Master,' said the boy, shyly. 'I caught these fish. And my mother baked the bread.'

'I am glad you brought them and gave them to me,' said Jesus, smiling at the small boy.

When everyone had eaten what they wanted, Jesus called His disciples and told them to go round and pick up all the scraps.

Nothing must be left to litter the lovely hillside and spoil it. The little boy went with the disciples, filling his own small basket with the scraps of bread and fish thrown down on the grass.

He looked at the baskets that were filled and counted them. 'Twelve!' he said. 'Twelve baskets full of scraps. And yet I only brought my own small

basketful. Truly this is a very wonderful miracle. What will my mother say?'

It was time for everyone to go home. The sun had set and soon it would be very dark. Jesus was in need of rest, and He wanted to pray to His Heavenly Father. He went silently into the hills alone.

The boy watched Him go. He had seen Jesus. He had listened to His stories. He had helped Him by giving Him his food. Jesus had smiled at him and spoken to him. He was the happiest boy in the world!

Now he must tell his mother all about it. She would hardly believe him! He ran up the hilly paths, panting. He was tired but very happy.

He came to his house at last. His mother was anxiously looking out for him. He flung himself on her.

'Mother, I saw Him! I saw Jesus! And do you know what happened to the five little loaves you baked, and the two fishes you pickled for me? Jesus took them and broke them and blessed them

– and Mother, there was enough to feed five thousand people! I saw a miracle done with my own bread and fishes!'

He told the wonderful story over and over again. 'I shall never forget this day,' he said. 'It's been the greatest day of my life!'

The Good Samaritan

This is a tale of great kindness. It is one of the best of all the tales that Jesus told. He was always preaching kindness and love, and in this story He tells us of a kind and good man.

Once upon a time there was a man who had to travel along a lonely road through the mountains, on the road that goes from Jerusalem to Jericho.

As he went along, robbers saw him. They had their hiding place among the rocks, where they waited for lonely travellers to come by. They pounced upon the man and caught him.

He shouted for help. He struggled and tried to beat them off, but there were too many for him.

'Take his money, his goods – and his clothes, too,'

said the chief of the robbers. They hit the poor man again and then left him, carrying off his clothes as well as his money.

The man was too badly hurt to walk. He could only lie by the roadway, groaning in pain. 'My head is bleeding!' he moaned. 'I shall die if I am left here without help. If only someone would come by!'

At last he heard the sound of feet. The wounded man lifted his head and saw to his joy that it was a priest of God who was coming by. 'Help!' he cried, feebly, 'Help!'

The priest saw the man. He did not go to look at him. He crossed to the other side of the road and went on his way. The wounded man could hardly believe that anyone could be so cruel.

Then someone else came by. This time it was a Levite, a man often in the Holy Temple, who worshipped God and prayed to Him. Ah, he would surely help!

The Levite went to look at the wounded man. He saw that he had hardly any clothes and that he had been robbed and wounded. But he did not help the man at all. He went calmly on his way and forgot all about the wounded traveller.

At last the man heard footsteps once more. He saw a man from Samaria, a Samaritan. The wounded man was disappointed.

'I have always heard that the Samaritans are mean and selfish,' he thought. 'Why, the priests and the Levites think themselves better than the Samaritans, and would not even sleep in the same house with one of them. This Samaritan will not think of helping me.'

Now the Samaritan was riding on a little donkey, his eyes on the road ahead. He suddenly saw the man lying by the roadside. He rode right up to him.

He saw at a glance that the man was badly hurt, and had been lying by the road for a long time.

'Poor fellow!' thought the Samaritan. 'Robbers have set upon him and robbed him. They have beaten him cruelly. I must do something for him. What can I put on his wounds?'

In his luggage, strapped on the donkey's back, were some bottles of oil and wine. The Samaritan got them and rubbed some on the man's wounds as gently as he could. Then he bound them up with strips of clean cloth.

'Do you feel better now?' he asked the man. 'Can you walk to my donkey if I help you? You shall ride him, and I will hold you on as I walk beside you.'

The wounded man managed to get on the donkey's back. The Samaritan clicked to the little beast and he moved off. The Samaritan had to hold the man firmly on the donkey, because he was so weak with his wounds.

But he was happy again. He kept looking in wonder at the Samaritan. How wonderful to know there was such kindness in the world! How marvellous to find someone so full of pity and mercy! The man could hardly believe it.

They came to a roadside inn. The Samaritan called to the innkeeper.

'Have you a good room and bed for this poor fellow? And have you any clothes? I will look after him tonight. I must bathe his wounds again and see that he has a good meal.'

He put the man to bed and looked after him. In the morning the wounded traveller felt much better. The Samaritan went to the innkeeper.

'I cannot stay longer,' he said, 'or I would see to this man. You must look after him for me. Here is some money. Take care of him till he is better and can go home.'

'Yes, sir. You can trust me to do that,' said the innkeeper.

'If you have to spend more than I have given you I will repay you when I come back this way again,' said the Samaritan. He said goodbye to the traveller, mounted his little donkey and went on his way.

'Now,' said Jesus, when He had finished telling this story, 'who can tell me which of the three travellers – the priest, the Levite, or the Samaritan –

was a kind and good neighbour to the man who fell among thieves?'

I shall not tell you the answer. I am sure you know it yourself, and will always be a kind and good neighbour to anyone in trouble.

The Boy Who Left Home

'Jesus has some strange friends,' the people sometimes said to one another. 'He does not always go with good men and women, as surely a good man should.'

Jesus heard what they said. He was sad. Did not the people know that God had love even for sinners and was grieved to know that they had wandered far away from the kingdom of heaven, far away from His love? Did they not see that He too must love sinners and go to try and bring them back to God again?

'I will tell them another story,' thought Jesus. 'There shall be three people in my story – a good son, a bad son, and a father who loves them both.'

And so He told the listening crowd this story, which is one of the loveliest He ever imagined.

There was once a rich man who had two sons. The boys had everything they wanted – good clothes to wear, fine food to eat, money to spend, and servants to wait on them.

But the younger son soon grew bored with his life on the farm. 'I want to go to the town and spend my money there,' he said to his father. 'There is nothing to do here and life is very dull.'

He was so bored that he would not work. He was idle and bad-tempered, and made his father sad. He laughed at his elder brother, who worked hard and did all that his father told him.

One day the younger son went to his father.

'Father,' he said, 'let me go away. Give me my share of the money, and I will go to the city and live there. You have my brother to work for you. Let me go.'

The father was sad. He gave his younger son his share of the money, and said goodbye to him. The younger son was pleased and excited. He set off in his finest clothes, singing, thinking of all the money he had with him. What a fine time he would have!

He came to the town and looked for lodgings. As soon as the people saw that he had plenty of money they came round him at once. He was pleased to see that he had so many friends. Ah, this was a fine life – he could give parties every day if he wanted to, he could buy himself the grandest clothes in town, and could eat and drink from morning to night.

But alas! – Money does not last for ever. One day the boy found that he had none left – and when his money went, his fine friends melted away too. They had only come round him because he was rich.

The youth was in a far country, where he knew nobody. What was he to do?

'I must get some work,' he thought. 'I shall starve if I do not earn money to buy food.'

But it was hard to get work. He had always been idle and he did not know how to work hard. To make things worse a great famine came to that land, and there was very little food. Most people were hungry, and a good many of them were starving.

'I am faint with hunger,' said the youth. 'I have never felt like this before. Somehow I must find work to do!'

At last he found a task. 'You can look after my herd of pigs,' said a farmer. So the boy sat under a tree, watching the grunting, greedy pigs.

'I am so hungry that I could eat the empty pods and husks that are thrown to these pigs,' he thought.

'How foolish I have been! Why, in my father's house even the very lowliest servant gets enough bread to eat – and here am I envying the pigs their husks!'

He sat and thought of his father's house and the busy, well kept farm. He remembered the feasts his father had given, the fine clothes he had worn, the friends he had had, and the great kindness his father had always shown him.

He was very homesick and very lonely. He told the farmer he could no longer watch his herd of pigs.

'I shall go home!' he said to himself. 'I am sorry

and ashamed. I will go to my father and I will say to him: 'Father, I have done wrong in God's sight and in yours too, and I am no longer worthy to be called your son. Make me one of your servants and I will work hard for you.'"

He walked many many miles to get back to his home. He was footsore and very tired. He was dirty and his clothes were in rags. He looked very different from the happy, finely dressed youth who had ridden away from the farm the year before.

His father had not forgotten him. Each day he had thought of him and prayed for him. He had looked for a letter from him but none had come. Every night the old man wondered what his lost son was doing, and whether he was happy or not.

Often he climbed up to the flat roof of his house just to see if by any chance the boy was coming home. 'If he is a mile away I shall still know him!' thought the father.

And then one day he saw someone in the far distance that reminded him of his son. But no, surely this poor, ragged, miserable youth was not his beloved son?

'It is my son,' said the old man, at last, and he ran with great joy to meet him. All the way he ran, and took him in his arms and kissed him.

'Oh, my father!' said the son in great happiness. 'Father, I have done wrong in God's sight and in yours, and I am no longer worthy to be called your son.'

The old man did not let him say any more. He called to his servants.

'Get the best clothes we have in the house, and put them on my son,' he said. 'Get a ring for his finger too, and shoes for his feet. We will have a great feast tonight, so fetch the calf that is being fattened, and kill it for our supper. We will eat and be merry, for this son of mine I thought was dead is alive again; he was lost, but now he is found.'

The youth was almost in tears. Everyone welcomed him, everyone was kind to him. How could he ever have been so foolish as to leave his home and family?

But wait – there was one person who was not pleased to see him back. The elder son was angry to hear that his younger brother had come home again and was being feasted and welcomed. He would not go to the feast.

He spoke angrily to his father. 'Have I not worked for you all these years and obeyed you in everything?' he said. 'But you did not give me a feast!'

'Son, you have been always with me, sharing in all the good things I can give you,' said the father, gently. 'You have lacked for nothing. It is right that we should welcome your brother, and rejoice. We thought him dead, but he is alive; he was lost, but now he is found. We must make merry and be glad!'

The Last Supper

Judas was one of the disciples of Jesus. He was clever, and the others trusted him to do many things for them.

'You can go and bargain in the town for the food we need,' they said to Judas. 'We have very little money and you can make the best of what we have. You are good at dealing with money and keeping account of it.'

Judas was a strange man. Although he was one of the disciples, he did not love Jesus. The only person he really loved was himself.

At first he had believed in Jesus, and thought He was a very wonderful man, so powerful that it would not be long before He became a king.

'And when He is King, He will remember all His disciples and friends,' thought the cunning Judas, 'and I shall be among them. I shall become a prince, at least! I shall have much power and a great deal of money.'

The months went by and Judas found that Jesus was certainly not going to be the kind of King that Judas imagined. And what was this kingdom that Jesus so often spoke of? It wasn't a real kingdom with palaces and soldiers and courtiers and plenty of money flowing in – it was simply a kingdom of love, to which the poorest of the land could belong.

Judas was scornful of such a kingdom. He had not given up his work to follow Jesus for that!

'This man is full of a strange power. He can work the most wonderful miracles,' thought Judas. 'Then why does He not work miracles for Himself and for us? He could so easily make us rich and strong and powerful! But He doesn't. He simply goes round talking and preaching, and healing the sick. I wish I had never followed Him!'

The traitor said nothing to the others of what he thought. Then one day he became afraid. Some of the powerful men of Jerusalem, the Chief Priests, the Scribes and the Pharisees, were making threats against Jesus. They were angry because the poor people loved Him, followed Him and believed every word He said. They were jealous and bitter.

Judas knew this. He knew that if the Chief Priests could take Jesus and throw Him into prison with His disciples, they would be glad.

'I don't want to go to prison,' thought Judas. 'I must look after myself. I will go to the Chief Priests and tell them I will help them to capture Jesus, if they will pay me. Then I shall be safe.'

Now it happened that Caiaphas, the High Priest, was calling a meeting of the rulers of Jerusalem to decide how they could take Jesus and put Him into prison.

'We will capture Him as soon as we can,' said Caiaphas. 'But not just yet. There is a great Festival in Jerusalem this week, and the town is full of people who love Jesus. We will wait till the week is over, then we will see what we can do to take this man.'

Someone came into the room where they were holding their meeting, someone who made the priests stare in amazement.

It was Judas – Judas, one of the very disciples of the man they had been talking of. What did he want?

He soon told them. 'I will help you to capture Jesus,' said Judas. 'How much will you give me if I do?'

This made things very easy for the priests. They were delighted. 'We will give you thirty pieces of silver!' said Caiaphas. 'That is the price of a slave, and is good pay for you.'

'Pay me now,' said Judas. He didn't trust anyone because he was untrustworthy himself. The priests counted out thirty pieces of silver for the traitor.

'I will send you word when you can capture Jesus,' said Judas. 'I will choose a time when there are few people about to interfere.'

Then he left the meeting with the money in his bag – and with a terrible secret in his heart.

'Nobody guesses what I have done,' he thought. 'I have sold Jesus for thirty pieces of silver. I am rich!'

But Jesus knew what he had done, and He was grieved and sad at heart.

It was Festival Week in Jerusalem. The sacred Feast of the Passover was being held. Jesus wanted to eat the Feast for the last time with His disciples, before He was betrayed by Judas.

'Go and prepare the Feast in a room I will tell you of,' said Jesus to Peter and John. So the two disciples went to the room that a friend had lent to Jesus for the feast, and got it ready.

Round the table were drawn couches, for in those long ago days people lay on couches to eat their meals and did not sit on chairs. The feast was of bread made without yeast, roast lamb, a sauce, a bitter salad, and wine to drink. Peter and John prepared everything ready for the meal.

Some of the disciples wanted to take the chief seats at the table. Jesus saw this. Had they still not learnt that such things did not matter? How could he show them that it was wrong and foolish always to try and get the best seats, the finest food, the most attention?

Now, usually at a feast there was a servant who welcomed the guests, and brought water to wash their dirty, dusty feet. But there was no servant that night.

'I will be their servant,' thought Jesus. 'I will show them that although I am called Master by them all, I am their humble and loving servant too, as we all should be to one another.'

He took off his long cloak and wide belt, and tied a towel round His waist. He took water and poured it into a basin on the floor. And then Jesus went from one disciple to another, washing and wiping their feet.

The disciples were astonished. Peter tried to stop Jesus from washing his feet, but when Jesus said, 'He that would be chief among you shall be servant of all,' he and the others knew what Jesus meant, and they were silent.

The great Feast began. Jesus broke the bread and blessed it, and then gave it to His disciples. He handed them the cup of wine, bidding each one drink of it.

He told them that the broken bread and the red wine were like His body, which would be broken, and like His blood, which would be spilt.

'This is my body, and this is my blood,' He said.

Then He told the disciples that He was soon to die, but that He would come again to them before He went up to His Father in Heaven.

And still we keep this Feast ourselves and call it the Holy Communion, eating bread, drinking wine, and remembering how Jesus gave His body and His blood for all of us who welcome His kingdom of love. It is our Feast of Remembrance, our way of coming close to the Lord and Master.

* * *

When Jesus and His disciples had finished their supper – the last one that Jesus had with them – Judas slipped away.

The time had come for him to betray Jesus. It was dark. Judas knew that soon Jesus was going into the lonely Garden of Gethsemane with His disciples. It would be a good time for the priests to send and take him.

Jesus waited until Judas had gone. Then He gave His disciples a new commandment – the very greatest and most important of all His commandments.

'I give you a new commandment,' He said. 'Love one another.'

He did not give it only to His disciples. He gave it to us as well. It is a commandment we should never forget.

Then Jesus arose and took His disciples to the quiet Garden of Gethsemane. He left all but Peter, James and John at the gate. He wanted these three near Him, because He was very sad.

He knew that His work on Earth was finished, and

that soon some very terrible things would happen to Him. Judas had gone to betray Him. Jesus needed to pray and to get courage and comfort from His Heavenly Father. Although He was the Son of God He was also the Son of Man, and He felt the same things that we feel, and suffered pain and unhappiness just as we do.

'Wait here and keep awake,' He said to the three disciples, and He went a little way away to pray.

After a while He went back to His disciples, feeling lonely and unhappy. They were all asleep.

'Could you not keep awake for me one hour?' said Jesus, sadly, and once again He went to pray to God. He knew that in a very short time Judas would come with soldiers to take Him.

Jesus went to His disciples twice more – and at the third time His face was full of courage.

'Rise!' He said. 'Let us be gone. Our betrayer is here.'

Judas had been to Caiaphas. 'Go now to the Garden of Gethsemane,' he said. 'Jesus is there with His

disciples. It will be easy to take Him there, in the dark of night.'

There came a noise at the gate, and in marched soldiers, priests, servants and the Temple Guard. They were armed with sticks and swords. They carried torches, and the flames lighted up the olive trees in the Garden.

'Judas, how shall we know which man is Jesus?' asked the priests.

'I will go to Him and kiss Him,' said Judas. 'You must watch to see which man I greet, and take Him.'

Judas went straight up to Jesus, who was standing silently beneath an olive tree.

'Hail, Master!' said Judas, and kissed Him, as was his custom.

Jesus looked at him sadly and sternly. 'Judas, do you betray me with a kiss?' He said. Then He turned to the crowd of excited men nearby.

'Whom do you seek?' He asked.

'Jesus of Nazareth,' they answered.

'I am He,' said Jesus.

Peter drew his sword, ready to defend Jesus to the death. He struck out at a man nearby.

'Peter, put away your sword,' commanded Jesus. He turned to the crowd once more.

'Have you come against me as if I were a thief, with sticks and swords? You laid no hand on me when I sat each day in the Temple, preaching. But now your time has come – this is your hour, and the powers of evil must have their way.'

Then the soldiers laid hands on Jesus and took Him. And all His disciples forsook Him and fled.

Peter followed the soldiers and priests a good way behind. He was afraid. How terrible to see Jesus, so wonderful and so powerful in all He could do for others, being marched away like a common thief! Peter could not understand it.

Jesus had known that the bold, impulsive Peter would be afraid. At the Last Supper He had told him something that the disciple had not believed.

'Although you say you would follow me and go

with me to imprisonment or death, Peter, I tell you that before the cock crows twice, you will three times deny that you know me,' He had said to Peter.

Now Peter, trembling and amazed, was full of fear as he followed the little company to the house of Caiaphas, the High Priest. He managed to get into the big courtyard of the house, and he went to a fire to warm himself, for he was cold and miserable.

A maidservant was there, and she knew him. 'You are one of that man's disciples, aren't you?' she said.

'Woman, I have never known Jesus,' said Peter, loudly.

Somewhere a cock crowed, for it was almost day.

Then someone else called out to Peter, 'You are one of the followers of Jesus.'

'Man, I am not,' said Peter at once.

And yet a third man said, 'Surely this man is one of Jesus's friends – hear how he speaks! He comes from Galilee, like Jesus!'

'I tell you I do not know this man!' shouted Peter, angrily.

Then the cock crowed for the second time, and Peter suddenly remembered what Jesus had said. He had said that Peter would deny Him three times before the cock crowed twice. And in spite of all the brave things he had said to his beloved Master, Peter had been a coward, and had denied that he knew Him.

Poor Peter! With a breaking heart he went out of the courtyard into the street, and wept bitterly.

The Story of Easter

Jesus had been captured. He was in prison, mocked at and scorned. His disciples had left Him, and He was lonely and sad.

Caiaphas the High Priest had ordered him to be taken to the Roman Governor, Pilate. Pilate would put Jesus to death! That was what the priests wanted – they must somehow get rid of this man whom the common people loved so much.

The Romans were rulers over the Jews. If only the Jews could think of bad things to say about Jesus, if they could say that He was planning to be a king, then Pilate would perhaps think Jesus meant to lead an army against the Roman rulers, and overthrow them to make Himself king.

'After all, Jesus has said he is king,' said the priests to one another. So He had – He had said that He was bringing them *His* kingdom of love.

'We will tell Pilate that this man sets himself up to be a king,' they decided, and so, shouting and yelling, they went to the court with Jesus and told Pilate the things they had determined to say.

Jesus said nothing. The Jews shouted continually. Pilate decided to take the prisoner into his palace and question Him alone. So he ordered Jesus to be brought to him, and he questioned Him closely.

He soon saw that there was no harm in this grave man with the steady eyes and clear voice. He would never lead any army against the Romans! He went out to the Chief Priests.

'I find no fault in this man!' said Pilate, meaning to set Jesus free at once. But the crowd were so angry that Pilate hardly knew what to do.

Then he remembered that Jesus came from Galilee. Herod the King ruled over Galilee, not Pilate. He could get rid of this man by sending Him to the

Jewish king, Herod. Herod was in Jerusalem every day. He could judge this man and do what he liked with Him.

So Jesus was taken off to Herod. Herod had heard about Him, and knew that He did many miracles. But Jesus did none for Herod. He stood there, silent, whilst everyone mocked Him, Herod too.

'You think you're a king, do you?' said Herod. 'Well, you shall be dressed as one. Fetch one of my red cloaks, and wrap it round this fellow!'

Then Herod sent Jesus back to Pilate, dressed as a king, so that everyone might see Him and laugh at Him.

Pilate did not want to harm Jesus, and he certainly did not want to kill Him. He did not find any fault in Him worthy of great punishment or of death. He thought that he would set Jesus free.

But the crowd would not let him. 'Do not set Him free! Set the robber Barabbas free instead!' they cried. 'Crucify Jesus! Hang Him on a cross and let Him die!'

Pilate set the robber Barabbas free, and gave orders that Jesus was to be beaten. The soldiers were cruel and merciless to Him.

'Does this fellow call Himself King of the Jews?' they said. 'Well, we will crown Him and give Him a sceptre, and a throne!'

So they gave Jesus a chair for a throne, and they made Him a crown of thorns that pricked His head, and they put a stick in His hand for a sceptre. They mocked at the poor, tired Jesus and had no pity for Him.

In the prison with Jesus there were two other prisoners. They were robbers, and they too were to hang on crosses with Jesus.

Each of the prisoners had to carry his own heavy cross. Jesus had His over His shoulder, and He could hardly drag the weight along, for He was tired and had been beaten by the soldiers. He fell down, and the soldiers had to take someone from the crowd to carry His cross for Him.

The guards took the three men to a hill outside the

city called Golgotha. There they fastened the men to their crosses and let them hang there for all to see.

People mocked at Jesus as He hung there in the hot sun, thirsty and in great pain.

'Ho! You have many a time saved others! But now you can't even save yourself!'

Some of Jesus's friends came there, and His mother Mary stood near, weeping bitterly. How could this happen to her good and noble son, at whose birth all the angels in heaven had sung?

Jesus was sad for His mother. He spoke to John, the disciple He loved most of all.

'Behold your mother!' He said. Then He spoke to His mother. 'Behold your son!'

They both knew what He meant, and from that day John looked after Mary as if she were his own mother.

Jesus was a man like other men, and He had to bear the same pain that the two robbers bore, and to feel the same great fear and unhappiness. He felt almost as if God, His Heavenly Father, had forsaken Him. It was His darkest hour.

Then He knew that He was about to die, and He cried out, 'It is finished! Father, into your hands I entrust my spirit.'

Jesus of Nazareth was dead.

There came a man called Joseph of Arimathaea. He was a friend of Jesus, and he wanted to take Him down from the cruel cross, and put Him in a tomb in a beautiful garden.

Pilate said he might take Jesus, and Joseph wrapped the poor, ill-used body in sweet-smelling linen into which fragrant spices had been put. Then he took Jesus to the cool cave in the garden where no one had ever been buried before. He laid Jesus there, and then left the tomb sadly, rolling a heavy stone across the entrance to seal up the doorway.

Some women who loved Jesus saw where Joseph had put him. 'Let us come here again as soon as we can,' they said to one another. 'We can do so little for Jesus now – but we can bring sweet spices to

the cave and anoint Him, remembering Him with love and grief.'

So, early in the morning of the third day, these women set out for the garden where the tomb of Jesus was.

'I saw where the cave was,' said one woman. 'There is a big stone to seal the doorway.'

'Shall we be able to move the stone?' said the other women, in dismay. They entered the garden and went to the tomb.

There was no stone in front of the cave! Someone had moved it. The women were full of astonishment, and they went fearfully inside the cave.

The body of Jesus was gone – but there, sitting in the tomb, was what they thought was a young man, dressed in a long and dazzling white robe.

All the women looked at him in fear and wonder. Who was this beautiful young man? Where was the body of Jesus?

The young man saw their fear. 'Do not be afraid!' he said. 'Are you looking for Jesus of Nazareth, He who was crucified? He is risen. He is no longer here. See, here is the place where His body lay.'

The women trembled, thinking this young man, so strange and dazzling, was surely an angel. He spoke again.

'Go on your way,' he said. 'Go to the disciples of Jesus, and tell them that Jesus will go before them into Galilee, and that they will see Him there.'

The women could not say a word. They fled away from the cool dark cave, which was so strangely lighted by the angel, and hurried out of the garden.

'Jesus has risen from the dead! Can it be true?' they said. 'Was that an angel? He looked like one. What strange words he spoke! Jesus is gone from there, that is plain. Where is He? Has He come to life again?'

They went to the disciples, who had all hidden themselves away in Jerusalem, afraid that they might be caught and punished too. They were frightened, puzzled and unhappy. How could their beloved Master have died such a terrible death? Was He not the Son of God?

The women came to them, panting out what they had seen and heard. 'Jesus has risen again!'

The disciples were full of the utmost amazement and gladness. Could this really be true? Peter and John could not wait for a moment. They ran off to the tomb in the garden as swiftly as they could.

John got there first. He stooped down and looked into the tomb. The angel was no longer there. The body of Jesus was not to be seen. Only the grave clothes were there, the garments in which Joseph of Arimathaea had so lovingly wrapped the dead Jesus. They were neatly folded in a pile.

'See, Peter,' said John. 'The women spoke the truth. Jesus has gone. He has risen again! This is glorious news.'

They both went into the tomb, marvelling. 'We must go back and tell the others,' said Peter. 'Did not our Master say that He would rise again in three days' time? This is the third day – and He has in truth arisen!'

'If only we could see Jesus!' said John, longingly. 'I would so much like to see our dear Lord again.'

One of the women who had fetched the disciples to the tomb was Mary Magdalene. She had loved Jesus very much, and when the disciples had gone, she stood weeping by the tomb. As she wept, she bent down and looked again into the cave. She now saw two angels there, one sitting where the head of Jesus had lain and the other where His feet had been. They spoke to her gently. 'Why do you weep?' they said.

'I weep because they have taken away the body of my Lord, and I do not know where they have laid Him,' said Mary, sorrowfully.

She suddenly felt that someone else was nearby and she turned to find out who it was, blinded by her tears. It must be the gardener. He would know where the body of Jesus was.

'Why do you weep?' said a tender voice. 'Whom are you looking for?'

'Oh, sir!' cried Mary, weeping still more bitterly, 'sir, if you have taken my Lord somewhere, tell me where you have laid Him, and I will take Him away.'

And then the man who Mary thought was the gardener said one word to her in such a familiar, loving voice that she knew who He was at once.

'Mary!' he said.

Mary looked up at Him, crying out gladly, her eyes suddenly full of joy.

'My Master!'

She knew that it was Jesus who had come to her, and she fell on her knees to worship Him, a great gladness in her heart.

For forty days Jesus stayed on our Earth. He went to His friends and to His disciples, making them glad, and telling them what they must do.

They must spread His kingdom of love, they must tell everyone the good news, they must teach, they must help the weak and the poor – they must carry on the work He had begun.

'You are the beginnings of my Church,' He said. They were the first Christians, the first of the many many millions who were to come.

And then, after forty days, Jesus came to the disciples no more. 'He has ascended to Heaven in a cloud of glory,' they said. 'But yet He is here with us still, in our hearts and minds, helping us just as He did when He was alive.'

He is here with us too, always ready to help and to comfort. He came down to this world to be one of us and to show us how to be good and loving, the most wonderful man the world has ever seen. And every year at Easter we celebrate this story, remembering how Jesus was crucified and rose again.

Echoing down the centuries that have passed since Jesus was born, nearly two thousand years ago, still comes His greatest commandment to us and to all men . . .

LOVE ONE ANOTHER.